Deliberate Wealth

The 5 Rules You Need to Know to Live Your Dream Lifestyle Today, Instead of Someday Maybe

Tyler Hoffman, FMA

CONTENTS

Preface—The First Pitch
Understanding "On The Court and in the Stands" .... *ix*

Rule #1: You Are the Source
Get a Mitt and Get in the Game *1*
- Raising Your Abundance Awareness
- Paradigm shift converter
- Wealth Mind Map
- Think, Feel, Act

Rule #2: Fear Doesn't Exist
Designing Your Dream Lifestyle. *25*
- Reverse Engineering
- Ignoring Fear
- Dream Lifestyle List
- Deliberate Action Plan

Rule #3: Cash Flow Is King
How to Finance Your Dreams *35*
- Pay-Split strategy
- Income Boost
- Deliberate Income Streams
- Freeing-up Money

Rule #4: Leverage Time and Money
How to Keep the Dream from Dying. *59*
- Time Blocking
- Stomping Out Multi-Tasking
- Using Other People's Time, Money and Expertise
- Becoming Financially Independent

Rule #5: Make Sure Others Get It
Enrolling others and Helping Friends *85*
- Sharing
- The Source of Fun

ॐ

Acknowledgements

To Rick and Pam Hoffman, my parents, who have always supported my endeavours regardless if I was the only one who could see the dream, and for giving me values and principles that enable my last name to live in high regard.

To my Brother, Brady, who is my best friend for life.

To my clients, who allowed me to believe in them.

And, to you, for wanting more from life.

Preface—The First Pitch

The first step to greatness is total commitment.
—Monte Holm

The coldness of the tile floor became slick as
each tear surrendered itself with martyrdom
from my now-puffy eyes. The tears caressed
my cheeks and trickled off my unshaven
chin, almost watery enough to drip onto the
travertine tiles below. It was 20 minutes past
6 a.m. and the only light that filled this hotel
bathroom was the day's first rays sneaking
its way through the thin curtains coming
from the Florida sun.

I was alone in the room but felt the need to
lock myself in the bathroom to hide my cries
from anyone who had ears. On my knees in
front of the bathtub, I lay for nearly 20 minutes, sobbing until my eyes were stinging,
and mouth dry, full of salt. I had never experienced joy at this level at any other point in
my life. Yes, I was happy. Elated actually.

If someone were able to see me, they would
think I had just lost a family member to a

sudden accident. The truth was my dream came true and, in this moment of realization, I could not contain my elation. For nine years straight, hour-by-hour I imagined this day and, in the last seven of those nine years, I literally consumed my existence with making sure this day played out as I desired, as planned exactly. This compulsion of achieving this day was a yearning for me, like lungs needing air. I innately needed this day with every ounce of my soul and carried out my life in every minute of those seven years creating it in my mind over and over, never losing sight, never settling and never leaving it to chance, ever. I never backed down.

I had just been told I was going to advance into the Major League Baseball's Umpire Development Program. I was awarded one out of eight contracts in the low minor leagues and I was to report to spring training in three weeks. Over 300 students from three umpire schools were after these prime opportunities. It was like getting the gold ticket on an American Idol contest, though I wasn't going to Hollywood, but to Scottsdale, Arizona.

All that I had sacrificed over the years gave birth to a new beginning. All the doubts that people cast were now a shadow behind me, fading into nothingness. My relationship with my word had proven to give me a great sense of integrity packed with conviction. I had arrived at the end only to realize that this was really the beginning.

When I arrived at spring training, the skies were high, the wind still, this April day in 1996. The air was highly electric; history was about to be made and I was going to set it in motion. I was all of 20-years-old and decked out in my new uniform. I had just rubbed up six-dozen baseballs with mud to take the sheen off the baseballs and had been visualizing my strike zone all day. My shoes shined up, I was ready to go. As I marched onto the field at Phoenix Municipal Stadium to umpire the first Arizona Diamondback's game in organizational history, I thought back to the time when I was 12-years-old umpiring for my mom's girls' softball team knowing that someday I was going to become a professional baseball umpire. The knowing was absolute, clear as rain, solid as a preacher's sermon.

The strange thing for me is that it wasn't just at 12 that I knew I was going to be a professional umpire; it was actually at the age of five. I was downstairs in my parents' basement one Saturday afternoon when the game of the week was on and I happened to be watching it. There was a really close play at first base and they showed the umpire make the call. The umpire who was kneeling on one knee came up and 'punched' the air like he was knocking out a heavyweight contender, calling the runner out. It was at that moment I knew what I wanted to be…I just didn't know how.

Growing up as a kid, I had my challenges. Being born several weeks too early, my ears hadn't fully developed which caused for a lot of ear infections. That led to having tubes placed in my ears three times, all before the third grade. This wasn't the half of it though. The severity of my ear infections had almost made me go deaf so, when I was learning to speak, my language development wasn't the best because I couldn't hear things half of the time. Instead of saying 'cookie,' I might say 'tookie.' To top it off, I had a lisp. Kids would make fun of me, I never let them know it bothered me but inside it hurt—no one likes to be made fun of.

In kindergarten I was ushered into speech therapy to correct my language skills. It was a struggle for me at first and attempted to rely on the word 'can't' to escape the hard work. That didn't last long though. Whenever I used the word 'can't,' my parents used to take me into the bathroom, stand me in front of the mirror, make me look myself in the eye and say to myself "I can, I can, I can." That exercise, coupled with the reading of, *The Little Engine That Could* every night before bed armed me for life. My parents believed in me so much, but they needed me to believe in myself. That simple exercise soon turned things around for me. I couldn't wait to go to speech therapy because I understood that the more quickly I learned, the more confidence I earned. I also learned that I could do anything I wanted to in life; it all comes down to a decision. Just like that little blue engine. That simple routine of standing in the mirror was the basis of my advancing into professional sports and taking on the challenge of writing and publishing this book.

Baseball is very predictable and built on a long-standing tradition. The first pitch is always at five minutes after 7 p.m. I could never figure out why it was never at exactly 7 p.m., but that meant that at about 7:03, the national anthem would start. Each night for five years, I would stand at attention, cap removed and placed over my heart, hands at my side slightly fisted as if I were holding two rolls of coins. My feet, heels together formed a 'V.' If a drill sergeant were watching me, he'd be most proud. For me, the amount of pride that filled my soul each night that anthem was sung spilled through my skin giving me visible goose bumps. At exactly 7:03 p.m. every evening, I had arrived. It was like a gold medal winner standing on the podium. The best part was when I woke up the next day I was able to relive the dream all over again. Except for one morning.

I woke up this one time and the day was different than the thousand that came before it. I knew the ticket I had been gifted for this special ride was no longer valid. I had recognized that all this particular career was giving me was a pay cheque every two weeks and an inflated ego. I was not having an impact on others and barely knew who I was, often giving into my values to feel accepted by my peers so I could advance closer to the major leagues and the good life of $250 per diem versus my then $15, and five-star hotels instead of the Econo Lodge.

Oh, and the crowds, the roar that pulsates in your heart. Living out of a suitcase, on the road in a new city every four days for five years wasn't for me. I belonged only on the professional field and not on the road.

Between the lines my life was solid; outside them, my life offered me a blurry vagueness that clouded my happiness. I was bored, unchallenged and lonely. I couldn't have the field without the road so I was done and it was time to for me to move on. I had to be the source of the change.

What does all this have to do in creating your dream lifestyle and building wealth? Well, everything actually. Sometimes we need other people in our lives to help us understand where we are and where we need to go. After all, we don't know what we don't know we don't know! Read that again a few times and it will sink in.

For me when I was young, it was my speech therapist and my parents. We are not born full of knowledge and understanding. I have a passion for helping others, which is why I left my professional baseball umpiring career. As I already mentioned, the career was only giving me a pay cheque every two weeks and an inflated ego. Both aren't bad, but when that's all you're getting out of a career, it's time to move on. Since 2000, I have educated myself so I can educate others like you.

My whole goal is to get you to shift your thinking so that you can make informed decisions so that you and your family can end up with living the good life right now and through retirement. My track record in life speaks for itself, and the skills I have learned and the thinking I have mastered are all transferable.

We have been sold a deferred life by 'the man.' Save for later, live the good life some day, maybe. Screw that, and never back down from the pursuit of living a front-end loaded life. Put these systems in place today so you can live the dream lifestyle now and still retire wealthy later!

The creation of your dream lifestyle is a much bigger game than the one you are playing now. It requires a tremendous amount of personal conviction, accountability and taking a stand not only for you but also for others. This book will create the possibility of you having it all, on all levels if you decide to play by the rules!

৵৽

Rule #1
You Are the Source

Get a Mitt and Get in the Game

Trust yourself. Create the kind of self that you will be happy to live with all your life. Make the most of yourself by fanning the tiny, inner sparks of possibility into flames of achievement.
––Golda Meir

You are the source to all that you are experiencing in your life right now and always. You are. Not the weather, not your job, not your wife or partner or husband. You are. Not your neighbour, your car, the meter maid, or your pet—you are. You are the direct source. What this means is that we are energy and we spin off both positive and negative energy and the universe just responds to that energy accordingly. Whether we want it or not, it comes back to us tenfold. Some call it the secret, the power of positive thinking, the art of intention, co-creating, and law of attraction. The science of being aware of your signals is becoming more and more mainstream as the quest to find the answer to the meaning of life and life's experiences become more closely examined. I like to think of myself as a radio and the station that gets played is the signal I am giving off...the radio just plays what I am attracting into it. If I don't like the song, I need to simply change my thoughts and feelings and a new song is played. Having awareness of this deliberate control puts you in the driver's seat of life. An excellent introduction to this is Michael Losier's book, *The Law of Attraction*. Get it, read and live it. Michael has played a big role in my personal development on this subject.

Knowing that you are the source, a sense of responsibility, or ownership should come over you. Human beings do not generally like to own their undesired outcomes or experiences. Instead, we like to blame others, avoid or deny that we are the ones to point the finger at. I remember a time when I was nine-years-old and I went into the fridge to pour myself a glass of orange juice. The lid on the juice container wasn't on tight and, as I was pouring it, the lid fell off and juice went everywhere, on the counter, down the cabinets and onto the floor. I remember throwing a tantrum and yelling in the kitchen, "Who was the idiot who used the orange juice last?" Laughing, my dad said to me, "Who was the idiot who didn't check the lid?" It's a simple example but so perfect to illustrate the point.

Instead of relying on other people to make us feel good, pay us high incomes or show us the way; we need to be the steward in our own lives and get on the court and out of the stands.

Where are you right now in your own life? On the court? Or in the stands? Are you just watching things pass you by, or are you down on the court making plays and hitting the ball? Seriously, I want you to really think about this for a second. Are you truly standing between the lines and in the zone or sitting in a box seat happily gazing at the activity below? When you run out of money two days before payday, are you blaming the rising fuel prices? If you missed your monthly sales target, is your first thought to blame your referral partners for coming up short this month? If you are late for a meeting, is it because of the traffic? Most people shift their shortcomings to people and things beyond them because then they don't have to take responsibility...it's the 'it's-not-my-fault syndrome!" Well, the cat's out of the bag and it's time to get real. As my mom would always love to say, "Get a Mitt and Get in the Game!" It is your fault. Though I don't like faulting people so let's substitute a word here. Let's trade the word 'fault' for the word 'creation.' It is your creation that you only have two weeks of vacation and not the four weeks per year that you would like. It is your creation that you earn $50,000 and not the $100,000 that you feel you are worth. It is you who are the source to all that you are experiencing and not experiencing in your life, wanted or unwanted.

So, you have two choices, keep focussing on what you don't have, aren't getting or feel you are missing out on. Or, instead, you can choose to focus on what you do want and are committed to doing and put yourself in the process of getting there. Once you 'put yourself in the process,' you begin with the end in mind and begin to deliberately create what you want. It's all about making better decisions. Essentially you can choose (decide) right now to live a powerful life or not. It's really that simple. You either commit to getting it done and doing it or you don't. These two different viewpoints create completely separate realities, my friend. So, if we have the choice, why not choose the more powerful one? You can invent anything for your life to experience.

The great thing is all you have to do is decide right now which reality you want to create for yourself. Most people's dreams are but only one decision away from being fulfilled. The challenge I see is that most people don't make the decision. Instead they'd rather stay in the story they created for themselves which is full of the past, rather than inventing a brand new possibility on the spot by looking to what is actually possible. And anything is possible; a shift in thinking and belief is all that needs to occur.

There are several easy exercises you can do over three days to shift your thinking, which will allow you to feel better about where you are and allow you to experience your dream lifestyle more quickly. You will need to get a notebook and make it your daily journal. Another item that will help you is to get a scrapbook or a large piece of poster board.

Day One

The first exercise is to increase your awareness of abundance and reprogram your thinking. Abundance is around us everywhere all the time, yet we often live our lives as if there weren't enough of anything. Many addictions are formed this way, needing more and more, more often. What I invite you to do today is to walk to work or take a walk on your lunch hour. The point is to get outside and observe. Keep your head up, don't look down—the sidewalk is going nowhere, you'll be fine! Instead, look at all of the leaves, the buildings, the cars and all of the beautiful faces. Make eye contact with as many people as possible and smile. Abundance is everywhere; experience the embracement of it all. Now, take this little exercise and apply it to all areas of your life. The next time you are getting groceries, renting a movie or at the gym, notice all of the healthy food, people creating work/life balance and the people at the gym who are in the process and committed to becoming fit. When I go to the video store and see that all 20 copies of the movie I want to rent are gone, I don't feel left out. Instead, I see a movie that is being experienced by a lot of people. This might sound corny, but my shift in thinking is always positive.

Chances are this viewpoint on life is considerably different than the one you have right now. By focussing on abundance and all of the positive things in life EVERYWHERE ALL THE TIME, you will attract this into your life always. You create from your source; you are the source, so create!

At the end of the day, write down what you noticed and saw in abundance and are thankful for. Many times I'd come home from a not-so-stellar day and wondered what the whole point of it was. By the time I finished writing in my journal, I had given notice to all that was beautiful that day which reminded me that life has really blessed me.

I encourage you to take this on in your life and not just do it for one day. This simple exercise of doing this before you go to bed will keep the positive thoughts, energy and emotion with you into your next day. It really will create a Zen-like state in your life. Imagine always paying tribute to what made your day great and life full. Delicious!

Day Two

Yesterday, you did a great job in gathering evidence of abundance. Today, we will take a different direction as I am going to share with you something I call the paradigm shift converter.

Download form on-line at www.deliberatewealth.com

Let's use money as a theme. Write down all the negative things you have to say or often feel about money right now:

1.   I have none

2.   Things cost too much

3.   My job doesn't pay me enough

4.   I have too many bills

Don't stop at four, keep going until you have no more. We shift the negative thoughts that hold us back by converting them into thoughts that are calls of actions that will actually get you closer to what you want. Remember, if you keep focussing on these negative thoughts, they will just stay constant in your life. When we convert these negative thoughts into positive ones, you put yourself in the process of having or completing, deliberately allowing you to experience all that you want in your life. Take a look and notice how you begin to immediately feel different in the moment:

1. I am orchestrating a plan that puts me in the process of creating wealth.

2. I relax knowing I have all that I need.

3. I am excited that my income will increase.

4. I love knowing that my bills always get paid.

The Words You Use

You'll notice the words we use in this exercise are much more powerful after the conversion takes place. By speaking in a powerful language, you will begin to attract even more of what you want in your life. Soon after I declared to my parents that I was going to become a professional baseball umpire, my mom would often tell her friends at social gatherings in my presence (all proud) that I wanted to go to umpire school and was hoping to become a professional umpire. I remember, I once stopped her and said that she was incorrect; I wasn't hoping to become a professional umpire, instead I <u>was</u> going to become a professional umpire.

There is a world of difference in that language. In one's life a dream is fulfilled; in another it's just a hope. Here are some other examples:

I will try to…. Instead use, I will do.

I need more _____ in order to…. Instead use,
I need _____ in order to….

It's a slight difference, but when we say we need 'more,' the word registers with our sub-conscious self that which we do not have. So, in the end, we are actually giving attention to the very thought we don't want to give attention to, the thought of not having and the universe responds to that so more of it keeps showing up!

Day Three

Another way to give positive attention to something we are wanting in our life is to construct a mind map. Essentially, we put down on paper all of the ways that are possible to experience or gather what it is we want.

Download from on-line at: www.deliberatewealth.com

Using money as a theme again and, staying with the idea of focussing on abundance, write down all the ways that you can get money to deliberately come into your life. Here are some examples:

- Scratch-and-win lottery
- Friend takes you for dinner
- Loose change in the couch
- Selling items on Craigslist.com
- Taking bottles back
- Bonus or raise at work
- Casino

Through the above exercises, we learned that whatever we give our attention to will grow or become more abundant. We needed you to give attention to that for three days so you see its importance.

Before I bought my Audi A4 convertible, I never saw one on the road. Now they are everywhere! The reality is they were always there; before, I just never paid attention. Same holds true if I were to tell you to look around and look for all the things that are brown. Do it right now and look around you. You probably never noticed them before but I am sure they stand out now. Our life is experienced in exactly the same way. Whatever we give our attention to, we will experience more and more of it. The challenge for most of us is that we wake up each day paying attention to the same things we did yesterday; nothing is different yet we expect different results.

Let's look at it in another light. If you ordered a steak and it wasn't cooked right, what would you do, keep eating it? I bet you'd send it back to have it cooked exactly the way you like it. A bad movie you rented, you'll shut it off. I doubt you'd force yourself to sit and watch it. So, what about your career, is it exactly right? What have you done about it? Complained? I hate my job, my job sucks, and my boss is a pain! How long have you been eating that 'steak' for? Tastes great, doesn't it? What about the relationship you are in or not in. My partner works too much and is never home; our sex life is terrible, and I can't find anyone who is engaging! Keep focussing on these and guess what keeps showing up. I don't even think I need to answer that, do I?

So, why is it that the trivial things in life like a steak or a bad movie we can just simply make a decision to get our pre-desired outcome back on track and the more important things in life like relationships, careers, money and fitness we cannot make decisions to alter the current course of the experience?

Exercise: What in your life are you ready to get rid of, move past and no longer want to experience? Make a list without judgement and create the possibility of having more of what you want and less of what you don't. By the end of this book, you will be living more powerfully.

Think, Feel, Act

According to one of the greatest influences of this generation, Anthony Robbins: "What we focus on determines how we feel, which usually determines the way we behave." Often in life we can turn to sports to draw a parallel understanding and, since I am an umpire, let's use this as an example. Whether it is from supervisors, fans or colleagues, sports officials are constantly being told to focus, concentrate and pay attention to something. It was put to me long ago from Bob Davies, the author of, *The Sky's Not the Limit— You Are!* that the way we THINK, affects the way we FEEL, which affects the way we ACT. Thus, the immediate thing one needs to address in any situation is their own thinking. For it is what's between your ears that keeps you from arriving at your desired destination.

Jim Evans, a leading worldwide educator for baseball umpires, says that focussing on positive thoughts alone is not going to produce a great performance. Evans says once a person has acquired and assimilated the knowledge, he then must manage what he knows. Rather than thinking about specific outcomes, think about each facet of your performance, the outcome will take care of itself. In essence, control what you can control and don't worry about the rest.

As both an amateur and professional sports official, it has been my 21 years of experience that too many officials become solely focussed on the idea of having an argument rather than immediately pursuing the avenue to have a professional discussion and diffuse the situation. Conversely, outside of the ballpark, many people focus on wealth and wealth only, without looking at how they want to experience the wealth and who they have to be to earn it and keep it.

A large number of officials lack fundamental principles such as understanding their respective rule interpretations and implementing specific game control techniques. They just haven't been educated properly or have not taken the steps to improve their own knowledge base. It's easier to yell back and not be a student of the game, than it is to work hard at becoming the best you can be. It's easier to watch what the guys on TV do and apply it to your game. There is no honour or courage in this method of application. The same goes in one's personal life. Without changing your game plan and adopting new principles, the same will always be played out over and over again, with no new results. It's easy to just plot along and cast blame as to why you're not wealthy, why your job sucks, why your partner holds you back and why you're overweight. They are all just excuses that have placed you in the stands instead of being on the court living the life you want.

The real courage is to gain experience through self-study (what you are doing now) by gaining confidence in your abilities through constant repetition in all facets of your life: money, community, fitness, health, sex, family and professionalism, a sense of inner calmness will exude. In the movie, *The Gladiator*, Maximus, *(The Spaniard)* exemplified the art of self-control consistently in each issue he faced. By controlling what he could control, he became a master in each scenario of disaster. He was able to identify each stage and option in every situation. He was then able to focus on the positive things to help him because he was prepared. All he had to do was draw on his experience. Imagine if he was a person in debt wondering about how the bills were going to get paid as he didn't have a job paying him what he needed! Where would he have ended up? Where would you have ended up?

There are two primary ways to control your focus, which will ultimately influence your ability to remain focussed on your goals. The first thing is to change what you are focussing on (what you picture, say to yourself and pay attention to). The second way is to change how you focus. Essentially dealing with the dimension of your mental picture. (Where do you see yourself, what does it feel like?)

By refusing to lower yourself to the standards of mediocrity, you will ultimately, with deliberate decision, begin to create your dream lifestyle. In every great battle a hero will always rise. While in an argument, Jim Evans makes it a point to intentionally remain calm and collected, not letting the other person's irrational behaviour dictate his own. "I learned long ago that when you raise your volume, you usually lower your IQ!" How we decide to react to life's curveballs will determine if you win the game of life or just stay a spectator and watch it all go by. Life is not easy; it is a game that requires steadfast devotion and constant vigour. The next time an unexpected bill shows up, watch how you react to it. When you need to spend more at a restaurant, notice your first reaction. When you have a dispute about money or what you want to do on your vacation, pay attention to this inner voice. Is it creating possibilities or intentionally disempowering the both of you?

Evans offers a prime example of a moment in his career where he was disappointed in his reaction to a situation. "Earl Weaver once got ejected from the first game of a Sunday double-header in New York. He came out on the plate umpire four times in the top half of the first inning. I felt he was making a travesty of the game but I did not intervene because the plate umpire was a veteran and was usually very adept at handling situations. As we were exchanging line-up cards for the second game, Weaver started to berate my partner and we ejected him simultaneously. He started to kick dirt on both of us. Instead of walking to the nearest grass area as I should have, I started kicking dirt back!"

The officials and people who choose to handle explosive or uncomfortable situations involving difficult decisions and difficult people are the ones who will excel in the game and in life. Maintaining your composure and staying true to yourself is arrived at by being fully and completely prepared before walking into the game. Proper and full knowledge breeds confidence. The way we think is dictated by what we know. The way we feel is tied to our mental makeup (state of mind or focus) and the way we act is in direct correlation to the two. The true dream lifestyle has you focussing on becoming better in all areas of your life and not overreacting when things don't go your way.

So many of us allow our thinking to hold us back. Our actions are often influenced by these four mindsets we take on from time-to-time. Can you identify with any of them?
1.   Not wanting to look bad
2.   Not having, or the feeling of lack
3.   Not feeling comfortable AKA Fear
4.   Not being true to our word AKA Accountable

For years, my brother was the guy in our relationship who never called, never invited me to do things, and was never really connected to me at all. We were close but not tight like we once were. I blamed him. The reality was that for so many years, I showed up in his life as the bossy big brother, the second parent in his life always lecturing him and telling him what he should and shouldn't do. I was oblivious to it all. My sermons to him were always meant well but when they fell on unsolicited ears they created a noise that caused him to not want to be around that and so he just avoided me. When I clued into this a few years back, it was like the clouds broke and the rays of the sun came through. I had an 'AHA' moment.

The payoff in my behaviour for me was that I got to be right, and we all love to be right, don't we? Being right is such a primal part of our being that subconsciously we are willing to ignore someone else's viewpoint only to stand our ground without even really knowing it. In the case of my brother and me, the impact on this was we were not as close as we could have been. Now it takes two—my brother every time he saw me recreated from his past experiences of me as someone who was bossy, controlling and talked about business too much. So each time he saw me he'd gather evidence to support his story so he could duplicate his previous experience and be right about me. We all do this all the time. The problem with this, is until someone has an 'AHA' moment and sees the light, shares the insight, acknowledges his/her behaviour and creates a new possibility, this cycle continues always and forever.

In order for the cycle to stop and a new one created, it takes for someone to have a breakthrough. For me the breakthrough was a question that was asked of me: **What is it about me that has my brother not being the way I'd like him to be in our relationship?** Once I had the answer. The only thing that was left was to share this with my brother. I had to come clean and acknowledge to him that 'yes,' I understand that I have been very parent-like with him and that the pay off for me was that I got to be right but the impact was that we were not connected because of it and the possibility I'd like to create with him was a relationship where we could be close and involved in each other's lives from this moment on. Did it erase the overbearing years of his big brother bossing him around? No, not at all. But what it did do was break the cycle and create a new possibility. One that to this day has allowed me and my brother to be tighter than we ever have.

That question can be applied to any area of your life. *What is it about you right now that has you not earning the kind of money you are worth?*

The Feeling of Lack or Not Having

If someone told you that there is nothing more or nothing less to experience right now other than what you are currently experiencing, how would you take that? For what you are doing in the moment right now is what you were meant to be doing. I had a friend (we'll call him Peter) who asked me to attend an Art Fundraiser with him recently. We were there for about 20 minutes and he turned to me and said he'd rather be doing the Grouse Grind (a famously popular steep and rigorous hiking trail in Vancouver) right now instead of being at this fundraiser; he was bored. So I asked him, **"What would have to be true for you to be enjoying yourself right now this instant?"** He looked perplexed, so I asked him again and he answered, "Well, if we had some interesting people to talk to, that would be a good start." I stood there quietly looking around at the 300-plus people, looking back at him, looking at the 300-plus people and then back at him. I did this four to five times and, by the fifth time, he got the point and, without saying a word, he headed over to talk to a group of women who were all too eager to greet his wide-eyed smile.

The feeling of lack or not having it comes from us not being true to our initial commitment(s). If Peter were true to his commitment, he'd not even bring up the fact that he was bored because he wouldn't have been. So, why didn't he initially follow through on having a good time? That brings us to the next distinction of not wanting to look bad. He didn't want rejection in a public place. This was holding him back. It was also holding back the ladies. Because of his avoidance, the group of ladies was missing out on meeting him too! The ripple effect transcends through all parts of our lives.

Not Wanting to Look Bad

A few years back I was doing some consulting work for a major international travel company. The president was routinely known for her pit-bull style of management—all numbers and no personal skills. It was all about results and not about the people. Because she was of the female gender, she didn't want her soft side to come through because she felt that was a weak sign of a leader. So she overcompensated. It wasn't until her reporting managers sat her down and created a new possibility for her that she clued into this and, within weeks, there was an entire corporate shift and all employees were able to create their own 'brightness of future.' Now, instead of just the president driving the company, 600-plus employees were all given the possibility to enroll themselves, or create their own future within the company. She 'not wanting to look bad' was stifling the entire organization.

We do this in our everyday lives, too. No one likes to ever look bad. The thought that you believe everyone is looking at you is a bit arrogant anyway, isn't it? We see this in fashion amongst teens where brand names play into social acceptance. Social acceptance comes in the form of agreements. For instance, there is a social agreement that if you drive a Lexus over a Pontiac you may have more money and your status is higher than most. You probably have a better job and know more important people. For many this pursuit of not looking bad is a trap to many financial woes.

I was working with a real estate agent a few years back who was called Cindy. As a real estate agent, she was constantly living in a world where having to look the part is a game all in itself. Or, at least this is what many real estate agents think. She told me this story where she was once working in the office and a nice couple visiting from out-of-town walked in and wanted to look at some properties they had been looking at for the last couple of days while visiting... they were wanting to buy a second home. Excited, Cindy offered to drive them in her car, a limited-edition Cadillac. As Cindy opened the door for the husband to get into her car, he stopped and said, with grace, that he'd rather work with someone who drove a jalopy because he knew they'd have nothing to hide. In sales, the transfer of trust is paramount. This was a humbling example and reminder that we don't always need to be trying to look good and that just staying true to your values is more important.

Not Being True To Your Word

Do you do the things you say you will do? When you make plans with people, do you stick to them or look for alternatives? How about personally—do you follow through with your exercise routine, diet or even things like wanting to travel or learn a new skill? Or does time, money and stuff get in the way more times than not? Have you settled for maybe someday? Newsflash, tomorrow will never come because you are not true to your word. If you expect to keep the same attitude and not change the way you feel about your goals and commitments, how can you reasonably expect yourself to achieve all the things you want to in your life?

Chances are, where you are in your life, your career, your relationship, is in direct proportion to how well you keep your word not only with yourself but also with others. One of my most challenging clients we'll call Ted, earns a considerable amount of money from his real estate portfolio. He had done what many aspire to by creating a portfolio that pays him six figures a year through passive income. He was always in and out of relationships, never consistent with exercise and always complained he never got to travel enough. Yet, he really had all the time and money to do so.

He had a different relationship with his word when it came to his work and personal life. I asked him if his success with his work and his relationships were reversed, what would he do differently to get his work back on track? He was quick to answer I'd block time off in my calendar to make sure I was spending enough quality time doing effective work. Then he got it, he was placing more importance on his work than he was with himself. He wasn't spending enough quality time with himself or others to feel that his life was in perfect balance.

Discussing this further, we discovered even though he blocked time off in the calendar to go to the gym, he would often work through that time slot, telling himself he had to work. The same thing showed for him in his relationships. Looking back, he saw that many times he'd have a dinner set up with a friend and would have to cancel at the last minute because something 'came up.'

Exercise: Think about the impact that your accountability with your word has had on your life and others both for when you don't follow through and when you do. Is there a common theme that shows up for you?

How you experience your life really comes down to how much you honour and respect yourself. In the context of creating your dream lifestyle, your accountability with your word is paramount to experiencing the fullness that life has to offer. It also requires a great deal of self-mastery and can be perceived as being the hardest skill on which to always deliver. We can look at this from several angles, so let's use two: time and money.

Being organized and planning your dream lifestyle takes time. It doesn't just unfold without deliberate creation and authentic intent. When I sit down with clients to check in on how well their Pay-Split strategy (explained later in the book) is working for them, on rare occasions they'd tell me that for the first few months they were doing great and then it all seemed to fall apart. They had every intention of using the freed-up cash to fund a business, save for travel or even retirement but, somehow, the money was gone, again. They said they would save but they didn't. I always ask them this one question: In spending that money that you said you were going to use for travel, and now you are not travelling, how does this make you feel? Invariably they see the impact of not being true to their word and change their future actions and thoughts.

Exercise: Life Balance Wheel

A very good little exercise is to use this life balance wheel. You can download this on-line from the free resources page at **www.deliberatewealth.com**. This exercise will show you where you needed to spend less and more time in specific areas of your life so that your life can become balanced. Without a balanced life, the pursuit of creating and achieving your dream lifestyle hangs in the balance.

Some questions to ask yourself that will help create clarity in getting more of what you want:

1.   What is the one thing I can do right now to feel as if though my life is balanced?

2.   If I had only two hours to create my dream lifestyle, what would I need to stop doing to realize that dream?

3.   If I felt no one was going to judge me, how would I really be living my life?

4.   If fear didn't exist, what are the three things I'd do right away?

5.   Am I spending my time with people that praise me for my self-expression or instead keep me repressed?

The truth inside these answers is what will set your dream lifestyle in motion. Not asking them, or even worse, not answering them is denial and will keep you shackled to what you don't want, a prisoner to your own life. For every answer I am sure you have a story about why you haven't addressed it or aren't taking action.

I am not interested in your story, for it is that and only that, a story. A story you made up to justify your inactions, your non-commitment, and your self-consciousness soaked in a weakness of fear. You need to hear the truth about what your stories in life really are—no sugar coating or honey—this is just how it is. Don't get interested in your own stories; get straight with yourself so your life is being lived more powerfully, more righteously, more mightily.

Rule #2
Fear Doesn't Exist

The Courage to Create

Life offers no guarantees…just choices; no certainty…but consequences; no predictable outcomes…just the privilege of pursuit.
—Tim Conner

ॐ∞

Choosing to Ignore Fear

Creating your dream lifestyle takes a level of courage. Courage is the ability to face your fears while fear can be contributed to the lack of knowledge or experience. So it would be fair to say that courage comes with confidence or, really, preparedness. Preparation is the key for football referee, Jimmy Harper. I had an opportunity to interview him for a feature story I was writing for "Referee Magazine" several years ago. Inside his conversation with me, he shared that he believes that it was through diligent preparation that allowed him to grow into the role of becoming a very well-respected football referee for the SEC Conference. "We had a situation years ago between Alabama and Tennessee. It was a questionable first-down play, which called for the chains to be brought out. Lots of emotion was everywhere.

It was my years of preparation, watching other officials, spending time with veterans, conducting pre-game and post-game conferences, as well as putting in time when I was younger, that gave me the insight into the game that allowed me to stay calm and talk the coaches down." This sports analogy is no different than real life. Your dream lifestyle isn't just going to show up one day out of the blue. It will and can only show up if you create it for yourself following a dedicated proven system.

When you are prepared, you welcome the challenges that others hope never even materialize. Jim Evans urges his students to think of tough situations as opportunities to prove their competence.

Accept no excuses, don't play into fear and leave no opportunity wasted. We often don't follow through with our dreams and goals because of the perception that we will experience fear, pain, rejection, embarrassment or loneliness. Do any of these really exist or are they all conjured up in our head? I believe fear does not exist. I am of the mindset that we create fear to keep us protected, even sheltered in a cocoon-like manner. Fear, or the reminder of a potential danger, (not yet emanated or realized) as I like to refer to it, keeps us sharp and focussed as we climb that ladder higher and higher or speed around the corner. At the same time, it doesn't allow you to enjoy the experience in its raw form. Fear holds you back. Appreciate the potential for what could happen if you don't pay attention, but create the reality of you experiencing what you desire beyond the fear that you have presented to yourself for, on the other side, is where your dream lifestyle lives in wild abundance!

You can choose the fear or choose the experience beyond the fear. Remember fear does not exist; you are the source of its creation!

Getting past this feeling is the first step into laying out the plans you need to create and win your dream lifestyle back. It's yours to win back. You had it all in the palm of your hand as a child and then as you grew older and placed your past experiences in front of you, time and time again; these new filters have slowly, over time, eroded that dream lifestyle from you.You will be faced with challenges, there will be roadblocks and they will either propel you to the next level or stop you dead in your tracks and hold you hostage in the land of mediocrity. So suck it up buttercup, dig in your heels take a deep breath, and enjoy the process of being a true champion.

Exercise: What are you really afraid of? Think about what is holding you back right now? Make a list of all the times you wanted to do something achievable but didn't— what kept you from realizing them? What can you do right now to realize them? If you realized them right now, how would your life be? See, by looking beyond the fear, you can see your dream lifestyle waiting for your arrival and that's what it takes to live a fully charged, amped-up powerful life.

Reverse Engineering

If you haven't already started to think of what you want your current and future life and financial situation to look like, I'd like to invite you to start a journal of where you will write down your dreams, perhaps paste pictures so you can create a really good visual representation of where you want to go. Refer to this book often and add to it constantly. You will find yourself paying attention to these things more often, making your conscious-self work towards these goals and visions you've laid out for yourself. You'll ditch the old-limiting beliefs, the thoughts of fear and rejection and, instead, leap towards what you have always intended your life to be.

Exercise: Create a scrapbook, cut images and words from magazines of all the key things you want and need in your dream lifestyle.

If you were taking a road trip, you would have in the car an atlas or rely on your GPS unit. Why leave your dream lifestyle journey to chance? The truth is, the more you connect with where you want to be, the more quickly you will get there—the more enjoyable the process will be and less stress will be created along the way.

Exercise: In your journal, make a list of all the things you want and need in your dream lifestyle.

Here is a partial list that I started when I was 15 of all that I wanted to do and experience in my life:

Be financially independent at 45	Learn to kite board
Umpire a National	Go paragliding
Become a professional umpire	Have a speed boat
Be the youngest professional	Own a home on the lake
Teach at The Academy of	Get published in several
Own a home before I'm 30	Write a book
Have a $1MM worth property	Become a professional speaker
Have a Jack Russell terrier	Have true relationships

When making your list, it's important to not second-guess yourself or come up with excuses like: I don't have the time for that or I'll never be able to do that, or that's too expensive. Just right down your top one hundred things you want to do, be, own, have, or experience. No limits, okay?

So, it's great to have this list but an idea without a plan will always remain an idea. So I am going to share with you some specific things you can do to achieve your dreams. I have been following these steps since I was a kid and they work every time. This book is a prime example of that.

Let's revisit my boyhood dream just for a second. My dream to become an umpire had been visualized over and over again in my head before ever actually getting there. I could see the stadium, hear the crowds and taste the dust. I also had a written plan down year-by-year on what I had to do to get to where I wanted to go and I enrolled others into my possibility. By sharing my goals, I gave myself the opportunity to be helped along the way allowing me to collapse time frames (get more done more quickly) and have my future come closer and closer to me. I talked to everyone in baseball I knew, read interviews on major league umpires. I even wrote major league umpires asking for advice. My dream was being shared; I wasn't keeping it to myself. It was because of my sharing that others helped get where I wanted to go. People cannot help you if they don't know what you want or are all about!

This is what it looked like when I was in the twelfth grade:

- 1993—Finish High School

- 1993—1995 Graduate from Sports Management at Malaspina University

- Umpire a National Umpire Championship and be assigned to home-plate for the final championship game, before going to umpire school

- Save up $5,000 for umpire school (work at marina, referee basketball games, sell advertising for map company)

- 1996—Attend Academy of Professional Umpiring and advance

- Attend minor league baseball umpire selection school and earn a professional contract

- 1996 Work in Short A (Make Winter ball)

- 1997 Work in Low A

- 1998 Work in High A (Make Winter ball)

- 1999 Work in High A

- 2000 Work in AA

- 2002 Work in AAA

- 2004 Be assigned MLB spring training

So, that's what I had; now each of those had their own mini-plans behind which I'll show you in a second. All of that became true right up until I left baseball by my own choice in 2000. So this little system works if, and only if, you are committed to your word and accountable to yourself for getting the job done. No one else can take the responsibility for getting it done or not getting it done.

If you were building a house, you'd need a set of blueprints. If you were retiring, you would need a financial plan. So here is a formula or plan template that you can use to achieve your dream lifestyle:

You can download the action plan on our website.

Dream Experience: Go to Bull Riding school

Expected Cost: $5,000 I want to experience this on: June 2011

I will share this dream with:

1.   My family

2.   My friends

3.   Other Bull Riders

Three things I can do today to put this dream in motion:

1.   Research the cost for Bull Riding schools

2.   Research flight and hotel prices

3.   Price out clothes and/or gear.

Three things I can do tomorrow to further advance this dream:

1.   Book a week off in June

2.   Schedule to have my assistant work that full week

3.   Share it with my friends and family

Three things I can do next month to further advance this dream:

1. Sell one thousand books to come up with the downpayment

2. Book five seminars

3. Start an on-line affiliate program to sell even more books

Rule #3
Cash Flow Is King

In the moment of a decision the best thing you can do is
the right thing. The worst thing you can do is nothing.
—Theodore Roosevelt

ॐॐ

Funding Your Dream Lifestyle

I have sat down with hundreds of families and individu-
als and too many of them seem to share the same thing in
common: they have no idea where their money goes and,
at the end of the day, there's not a whole lot left over to
save for retirement or even begin to have money put aside
to put their dreams in motion. They cannot save at the levels they need to save in order for them to retire wealthy.
Why? Simple, they don't follow through with what they
said they will do. And they are relying on one static stream
of income; their life experiences are capped by their income. Despite reading "Budget Traveler," one cannot live a
million-dollar lifestyle, be part of the jet-set on a $30,000 a
year income. You either need to go into debt or be committed, accountable and create new income streams. People
very often lack the integrity within themselves and are not

accountable. If they kept their word and were accountable they would have money left over.

My ears have heard this story over and over again: I can't afford to do that. Yet, they won't think twice about spending $125 on going out to dinner or dropping $50 in the night club. The worst one of all is the cable bill. Spending over $125 month on cable or satellite is foolish to me, especially if you are in the asset accumulation stage, meaning you NEED to be saving money.

If your life absolutely needs "The Apprentice" and "Survivor" or "Big Brother," then maybe you should try to get on the shows! Instead, get the basic cable and save $75 a month. How about your Internet package? Do you do a lot of downloading, or just use it to check your e-mail. By switching from a 'Nitro Fast Speed' cable plan to a basic speed, you can save over $30 a month. It all comes down to what are your priorities in life. If you save $30 a month ($1 a day), every month for 25 years it could grow to $28,531 assuming it could average 8%. If it averaged 10%, it would grow to $39,805. If you really want to have a wealthy lifestyle and experience life, then you need to get in touch with your 'why' and decide today that you will take action to achieving that goal.

The first step in the process of creating an opportunity for you to save money is to get organized and see right now where your money goes on a monthly basis. By visibly seeing exactly where your money goes, you will give yourself more control and pay closer attention. You can use the 'Cash Flow Calculator' by logging onto our website. **www. deliberatewealth.com**

Once you know where your money is going, it is the time to stop using your after-tax dollars to buy liabilities. A liability is something that comes with a sustainable price or requires money continually to keep it working. People often become financially burdened by their liability and wonder why they have no assets. What the wealthy do is buy assets that will pay for their assets. They buy investments that will grow to produce income streams to fund their dream lifestyle. Here's an example of how one of my clients planned on funding his future Aston Martin.

With the rental property he owns it will eventually be paid off as he has a renter making that possible for him. Once the mortgage is paid off, he will have new cash to put to work. I always have my clients keep their money moving so that it is constantly working for them. In this case he will borrow against his home and put the cash into an investment that will grow. He will also take out each month enough money to cover the lease of the Aston Martin, gun-metal blue with tan interior he tells me! The money that comes out of the investment I will set up for him so that is return of capital (his original money) so that it will be taxed less than if he were pulling out the gains to pay for his new lifestyle luxury toy. In the end he gets his toy in a tax-efficient way and will have two assets (condo and investment portfolio) growing at the same time making him even more money to fund his dream lifestyle.

This is just one way, and there are hundreds that a financial advisor who specializes in building and protecting wealth can create for you.

Some of my clients have bought positions into start-up companies and now receive either a nice monthly or quarterly pay cheque which covers the cost of their recreational property. Really you can be as creative as you want; the key is to change your mindset and recheck what's important to you and align yourself with people that can get you there. I'll share more of this with you in a few pages, along with a few simple strategies that can help you seal the deal on your wealth creation.

Lifestyle Strategy #1: Pay Split Your Pay Cheque

People's intention to save is always there but they often slide off because they are not following a systematic approach. You need to put systems in place to help achieve the goals you just laid out for yourself. There's no sense committing to your new dream lifestyle plan if you don't put some checks and balances in place to keep the momentum going.

This is where you need to be open to change. I can probably be accurate in saying that you have one bank account to look after all of your personal finances right? Your pay cheque goes in, you use the ATM to take money out, you pay your bills from this account and, at the end of the month, you may or may not be in overdraft and you're not too sure why, am I right?

Remember that little exercise you just did by showing yourself how much money you spend on each item every month and then we were able to determine that you should have X amount left over each month? I know you were looking at that bottom number and telling yourself there's no way I have that money left over!' 'I must have bought a few things!' Chances are, yes, maybe you did miss a small item…but the reality is for most people is that they do not have that money left over each and every month but because they spend it, unknowingly. They have one bank account looking after everything; they have no clue how much they have at any given time and the money just gets depleted over the month—$25 here, $10 there, it adds up. They know they just got paid, they know there's money in the account, so they spend…never thinking about where it goes. We live in an electronic world where we zap our card and whammo we have a purchase. It's the same technology that makes life convenient for us that keeps us out of touch. Imagine if you took cash out and put it in your wallet every week, you'd have a better idea of where it goes.

Using that same spreadsheet, you determined two important things: what your variable expenses are (daily living expenses) and what your fixed expenses are (bills, etc.) Your fixed payments are just that, fixed they don't change from month-to-month generally. The area that you do have control is on your daily expenses. Let's say you identified on the cash flow sheet that you need $800 a month to look after your food, toiletries, grooming, and entertainment, while your fixed bills require $1,500 a month to look after rent, the phone and utilities. So each month you need $2,300 to survive.

Instead of having all of your money crammed into one bank account each month, I am going to encourage you to have two chequing accounts. If you're worried about fees there are banks that have no fees. One account will be for your day-to-day expenses and the other account will be for your bills. Every time you get paid, you will have $400 go into your day-to-day account and $750 going towards your bills account. I call this simple little strategy, the Pay-Split strategy.

By splitting up your pay, you will be able to better track where your money goes. All you have done is identified what it is that you need to survive each month and have allocated a dollar amount towards that expense category. Instead of being on a budget, you have just put measures in place so that you don't overspend.

If, after ten days of being paid, you are out of money in your day-to-day account...you're going to have to wait until you get paid next. This is where the discipline comes in. I also encourage you to have your ATM bank card set up so that you cannot take money out of your bills account via the ATM machine...this will help you, rather stop you, from impulse shopping. Meanwhile, in your bills account, every-thing is happening automatically. If you do not have your bills set up to be paid on-line automatically each month, get your bank to help you do so. Doing this saves time and stress. At the end of each month you will have a surplus in your bills account, or should have. It is this surplus that you can use to pay down debt or use for the purchase of buying real estate, fund your savings or investment goals.

Now your employer may be able to split your pay up between different accounts so check with them as that will make it easier for you. If they cannot, simply set up an automatic re-occurring monthly transfer from one account to another. I recommend President's Choice Financial (CIBC) as they have no-fee banking and everything can be done on-line with ease, not to mention free groceries!

The Pay-Split strategy will make it feel like your finances are on a budget without having to track each and every purchase. Try this for 90 days and see how much money you are able to save each month. I guarantee that by cutting back on the areas that you have decided to cut back on and by implementing this Pay-Split strategy, you will be able to save an extra 15-20% each month with little effort.

It doesn't matter what it is in life, the first few steps are always the hardest. If you're starting out in sales like T. Weurth above, it might be picking up the telephone. If you're interested in someone it might be asking somebody out on a date. The thing is, once we get through it, everything is okay after, isn't it? It never fails, the moment we bust through the hardest task, the rest just seems easy. The same thing can be said when trying to amass a large sum of money to plunk down on your first home. Like a fitness model preparing for a magazine shoot, this is going to require some hard and steadfast discipline. It may even require you giving up a few things in order to create the dream lifestyle you want. In the end, you'll look back and appreciate the fact that you were able to get through the small sacrifices to have the home you always wanted.

Lifestyle Strategy #2: Grow Your Income, Just Add Courage

One of the easiest ways to increase your cash flow is to get a raise from your work. If you have not had a raise in two years, it's time to knock on your boss's door and have a conversation. Most companies give a living adjustment raise each year between 2-4% to keep up with inflation. This is not considered a raise per se as it has nothing to do with your performance and contributions to the company. Some tips to requesting a raise:

- Ask for a meeting in the morning so that not 101 things have gone wrong for your boss by the time you get to him or her.

- Don't waste time, get right to it. Be upfront and summarize how you've contributed to the company.

- Show your boss that you have vision and talk about where you'd like to go with the company.

- Request a raise of 25%—start high and work your way down.

- Prepare a one-page summary of your contributions since you've been hired, outlining your track record and impact on the organization.

- If you cannot get an answer on the spot, request a second meeting where you can negotiate; if you do not set a date, chances are there will not be one.

- Whatever the decision is always, always provide a thank-you card. Nothing too crazy like a signing telegram. Just a smart little card thanking him or her.

The extra money you earn from your raise can pay down debt and go towards your savings goals. By using the Pay-Split strategy, you will get accustomed to spending a certain limit. Even the wealthy spend within their means. You see this a lot within the Baby Boomer generation; so many are living in homes they can't afford and driving cars they can barely make the payments on. Living within your means is about getting accustomed to a lifestyle and saving deliberately so you can have the dream lifestyle you deserve. The wealthy own businesses and have assets that pay for their toys and, by following what they do, you can win the money game. The increase in your cash flow will create some temptations to go buy stuff. I encourage you to buy assets that will pay for your stuff and buy incredible experiences.

Lifestyle Strategy #3: Create Multiple Income Streams

This is my favourite strategy! Another way to grow your income is to look at starting a home-based business. This will allow you to grow your income and create some in-home business deductions thus paying less tax. Turn your hobby or interest into a business. To successfully create your dream lifestyle you will need multiple streams that deliver cash to you. Ideally these streams continue to flow when you're on the beach in Mexico, skiing in Whistler, kite boarding in Chile or having dinner in Hong Kong.

Creating automatic or instant income requires tools that allow you to conduct business while you are away. After all, I am sure your dream lifestyle doesn't have you housebound. Some of my favourites include:

Skype—an Internet phone program that allows me to call anywhere in the world and it's free to download at www.skype.com

OneBox—An on-line unified messaging service. All of my calls, e-mails and faxes get delivered in one spot keeping everything easy to find and I'm never out of touch. www.onebox.com

Go to PC—this let's me connect to my office computer from anywhere in the world, that client proposal I need access to is a click away. www.gotopc.com

Shopping Cart—delivers the purchased information products in real time and pays me everyday on the spot. It will also look after my newsletters and automatic reply e-mails keeping my business front and centre when I am not. This simple program makes me money on a routine basis.

There are a variety of ways to make money and many ordinary people are making good incomes doing these:

Ebay

If you already have products that you sell, then consider opening up a store and leveraging your efforts by having an on-line store with either Yahoo or EBay.

Informational Products

Another instant way to increase your income is to create and sell information products on-line. You can even promote other people's products and earn money.

By selling informational products on-line, you can easily create passive income while you sleep or while you work, all the while helping fund your dream lifestyle. Informational products can be in the shape of books, CD's, workbooks, manuals, audio books…the list is as endless as your creativity is.

If you are a sales or service professional, this will also help you establish more trust and credibility in your marketplace. But you don't have to be in the sales or service industry to produce informational products. Maybe you're an executive assistant that has some great tools and systems that other executive assistant or HR personnel could benefit from. Chances are you may not even have to produce them as you are using them already. Again, be creative and have fun, there's a market for everything!

You can increase the rate of your sales if you offer affiliates the opportunity to market your information.

Exercise: Make a list of things you could help people with, educate them on. What do you like to learn about or read or do that you could create a product for people to buy?

Affiliate Marketing

Affiliate marketing is like being a reseller. You don't produce the product nor do you process the order or ship the item. Instead you help promote the product or service through your existing marketing. If you don't have a business that has existing marketing, then some of the ways people promote their affiliate is through creating a website, starting a newsletter, writing articles and publishing them on-line and for magazines. Commission Junction is a great place to look for companies to represent as is.

You can even join mine. By sharing our products and systems you will earn 15% www.deliberatwealth.com

You can make easy quick money by selling this book and my other Wealth Systems! For more info or to get

the Deliberate Wealth Cash Course and make money on-line right now, go to: www.deliberatwealth.com

Network Marketing

Network marketing companies are a great avenue to pursue because they offer a system whereby you can just plug yourself in and they help you with every step of the marketing plan. They also have great training. Some examples are: Pre Paid Legal Services, Send Out Cards, Talk Fusion and Arbonne. We can even help you get started with these companies and place you with a team that is going to give you the support and direction you need. Just e-mail us at coach@deliberatewealth.com and we'd be happy to help you explore the right opportunities with you. These companies all specialize in their own niche market and have fantastic marketing strategies that you can access for literally only a few dollars which, as a business start-up cost, are tax-deductible. Network marketing companies offer the systems and brand names of a franchise without the start-up costs and royalties! Part of your rent/mortgage, utilities and automobile expenses could be written off against your income if you are using them to generate an income.

With the new income stream and tax savings, you will be able to create your wealth accumulation sooner.

Become a Home-Based Travel Agent

Almost every time when I talk about creating dream life-styles with people, travel is at the top of their list. The idea of traveling to exotic places and working abroad is easier now than ever with a global economy. The drawback is the cost. When you factor in flights, hotels and food even with points it can add up to be quite a bit.

People often turn to time shares, fractional ownership and vacation clubs in an attempt to save money. There is program called Primo Vacations that I have researched front to back, upwards and downwards and inside out and it's solid. The prices that they have secured for their members is ridiculous and the best part is you can even sell memberships and earn $500 for every sale...it's a total win-win opportunity. Send me an email today and I can provide you with information on both the product and business opportunity.

Here's an example, the Sheraton Buganvillas in Puerto Vallarta is roughly $850 for five days. With Primo Vacations, it's $295 for the four days. I've stayed here and I can tell you for a five star property this is a great deal.

Primo Vacations offers Resorts, Cruise Lines, Hotel Chains and access to every other vacation related service members at the highest level of quality (4—5 Star Resorts) at discounts you cannot get anywhere else.

Strategy #4:—Swap Bad Debt With Good Debt

If you're reading this and it's June and you still haven't paid off Christmas VISA bill then this strategy will make a lot of sense for you.

The idea here is to get rid of your liabilities while at the same time adding to your assets. Let's take a look at this as an example. Let's assume you have overspent your way to a bunch of maxed out credit and department store cards that looks like the following:

MasterCard at 19% with a $3,000 balance and paying $100 per month.

VISA at 19% with a $7,000 balance and paying $100 per month.

Department Card at 29% with a $3,000 balance and paying $200 per month.

Department Card #2 at 29% with a $2,000 balance and paying $200 per month.

In this case, you has a total of $15,000 in high-interest debt and Monthly payments of $600 in total. The total amount of interest being charged PER MONTH is $279.16. Calculating the interest you are being charged to carry debts on stuff that have long depreciated is a humbling experience. In this case, almost half of the payments are being directed to interest costs alone!

Let's assume that you were successful in asking for that raise we talked about earlier and are now earning $145,000 per year. This would put you in the highest tax bracket, which for Ontario is 46.41%. Since you have been playing catch-up with your finances, you have really fallen behind in their retirement savings so there is a lot of unused RRSP contribution room. Only about 10% of Canadians maximize their RRSPs!

If you could make an RRSP contribution big enough, the tax refund could be large enough to completely wipe out your high-interest debts! So what would be involved?

Well, we know that in this case you don't have the cash on hand; otherwise the high-interest debt would have been paid off long ago! So you will need an RRSP Loan. The first step is to calculate how much of a loan you will need in order to generate a tax refund equal to $15,000. An easy way to figure it out is to log onto Ernst & Young's Personal Tax Calculators. Simply GOOGLE: Ernst Young RRSP Calculator

It will give you a very good idea as to how much you will need to borrow and contribute to your RRSP to get a certain amount of refund! Just plug in the numbers until you get the desired refund. For this example, we arrive at the following amount of contribution needed for a $15,000 refund: $32,887.

The second step is getting an RRSP loan from an Independent Financial Advisor! Banks like to give you loans so they can sell you bank owned mutual funds. An Independent

Advisor can find the best investment solution for you in an unbiased environment. Ideally, what you want to do is keep your cash flow the same as before the loan, so you would like to find how long the loan should be for a $600 monthly payment.

Using a loan calculator we find that $32,887 paid back over 60 months (and assuming an interest rate of 7%) would be about $650 per month. That's close enough that it makes sense for this example...Now, before getting the loan, you will want to look for a loan provider that allows for a 3 or 6 month deferral on your first payment. The reason for this is that once you take out the loan and make your RRSP contribution you will have to pay for not only the loan ($650/month) but also the debt payments ($600/month) until your tax refund arrives! By having the ability to defer the first loan payment for 3 or 6 months you can eliminate the overlapping payments.

Hopefully you can see that the strategy does work by putting in a lump sum into the retirement savings now and by basically converting bad debt into good debt. But probably the best part of the strategy is the psychological lift you can get having a substantial amount of savings to kick-start your RRSP along with zero high interest debt to serve.

Strategy #5: Use Your House as a High-Yielding Savings Account

Every time you make your mortgage payment, you are creating a tiny bit of equity. Many people share the mindset that the best thing to do is to pay off this mortgage as quickly as possible and then either live in it with no payment or sell it for a big tax-free gain. That thinking does make sense if mortgage rates are above 10% like they were in the 1980s. Then they were around 20%. Of course, if you were paying 20% interest on anything, you would want to pay it down to save thousands of dollars. In today's world, interest rates are at an all-time low and the equity markets, though a little sluggish are performing and will continue to perform quite well as the boomers start to retire.

So, all of this means that homeowners need to adopt a new philosophy. For the first half of your mortgage, that is exactly what I want you to do—busily create equity in your home as fast as you can so you can use the equity later on in life to maximize this investment. If I gave you the choice of becoming either wealthy or financially challenged, which one would you pick? It's a no-brainer, of course. So, if you want to become wealthy, would it not make sense to find a wealthy person and just copy what he or she did? Of course it does! Ordinary people can create extraordinary wealth if they just copy what the wealthy people do. Financially successful people do not pay down their mortgage in the conventional sense that the rest of us are planning on doing. Instead, they create equity in their home, take that equity out and diversify it and get it working for them and create tax deductions along the way! I know what you're thinking: "Wait a minute, my banker never told me about that!" I know they didn't and that's exactly why 75% of us will retire financially challenged because we do not know what we do not know.

So, from the time let's say you're 20-40; we need to get you to create as much equity in your home as possible. Here are some key strategies that will enable you to do so:

- By using a variable-rate mortgage, you generally will pay less interest. Historically this is the case. For instance, at the time of writing this book, a variable rate mortgage is 3.45% while a five-year fixed is 4.80% and a three-year fixed is 4.5% Why pay $1.35% more? On a $250,000 mortgage, you would be paying $184 more a month in interest if you went with the five-year fixed. Another way of looking at is over the five-year term, you would have paid $11,040 more, assuming that the variable rate never changed.

- A very simple way of saving a lot of cash and time is to take an amortization of 15 or 20 years instead of the automatic 25 years that the lender 'gives' you. Lenders make the most interest on 25 years so, naturally, they'll sell that to you based on the fact that it will give you the lowest payment. Remember, in the first half of your life, we want to create equity.

By going from a 25-year amortization to a 20-year amortization, you won't have to come up with that much extra each month but will get more money going towards the principal. For some of you, you might even be able to go below 20 years.

Assuming a $250,000 mortgage @ 5%

Amortization	Principal Amount	Interest Amount	Monthly Payment	Monthly Difference
25 Years	$423.03	$1,030.98	**$1,454.01**	-
20 Years	$611.83	$1,030.98	**$1,642.81**	*$188.80*
15 Years	$939.33	$,1030.98	**$1,970.31**	*$516.30*

Just by changing your amortization from 25 years to 20 years (and assuming rates do not change over that time), you will save $2,265.60 a year or $45,312 over the length of the mortgage! By doing this, you will begin to create equity in your home that much faster.

Max out your RRSP's each year, borrow if you have to and take the refund that you'll be getting and plunk it down on your mortgage balance each year. Most lenders will allow you to pay down 15% of your mortgage balance in the form of a lump sum. If you are earning $40,000 and contributing the maximum $7,200 (18%), that means you will be saving roughly $2,068 that's an extra 2K that you slap on your mortgage. Over five years, you will have paid down an extra $10,000.

- Pay your mortgage weekly or bi-weekly. By doing this, you will save some interest costs. Just make sure that when you set this up, that your lender isn't just spreading out the usual monthly payment over the entire month; when they do that, you are no further ahead.

- Use the same strategies you used when saving for your wealth accumulation: get rid of any unnecessary bills that you don't genuinely need. Lower some of your service plans if you have to, like your cable bill and the Internet.

At the end of the day, you need to live and have a life, but if you can be disciplined enough to create as much equity in your early years as possible, you open a world of opportunity for yourself to really maximize your real estate. Your goal is to get a loan to a value ratio of 60% or better. Meaning, if your house was worth $200,000, you would want to create 60% equity in it by paying down the mortgage to $120,000 or better! Once you reach this LTV ratio, this is where you can begin to look at the next phase in your strategy.

Let's do a side-by-side comparison of what people who follow common logic do versus someone who deliberately wants to create his or her wealth.

Assuming a $250,000 mortgage.

Common Logic:
Five-year fixed over a 25-year amortization =
$1,426 month ($990 interest)
Deliberate Wealth Logic:
Variable Rate over a 20-year amortization =
$1,440 month ($714 interest)
By deliberately choosing to create your wealth, you will save $276 a month in interest, or $3,312 annually or $66,240

and five years (assuming the rates were to never change)—
this is a heck of a pay off!

**Lifestyle Strategy #6: Using Real Estate to Pay for Your
Kids' Tuition and Get Your Money Back**

It's becoming increasingly harder for students to come up
with the means to support themselves through college and
university. With rising tuition costs, many simply cannot afford to go unless taking on huge student loans. I always
encourage parents to create an education savings plan of
some sort as well as getting their own kids to save while
working part-time through high school.

There is one neat little real estate strategy that can work
quite well for you too and that simply is getting into the
dorm room business. Now, ideally, if your child can live at
home and go to university that would make the most financial sense for all parties. If they cannot due to distance
then this will work very well.

About four months before school is set to go back in, you
will want to buy a 3- or 4-bedroom condo or home near
the college you child is attending. The closer to the college
the better and the more rooms you can get the better. Off-
campus housing is always tough to find and is always in
high demand. The more rooms you have, the more rooms
you can rent out.

When signing the leases (never go month-to-month), make
sure you sign each resident on an individual 12-month lease

with the option to sublet if they are not going to be there in the summer months. By doing individual leases with their parents as co-signers, not only will you able le to attract the maximum rents but also hold everyone accountable for any damages. I would suspect you would be able to rent the rooms for at least $400-$500 depending on your area. Check around to see what other people are charging. The rents you receive each month should be quite adequate to cover the mortgage and property tax each month.

Each month you will find that you are probably just break-ing even or maybe even making a loss. This is okay—you can write the losses off and, at the end of four years, the property should have increased substantially in value be-cause of the location of your property.

Another aspect to this strategy is to have your child act as the property manager and pay them a small salary each month of, say, $100-$200 a month to help pay for books and food. So long as your son or daughter is doing legiti-mate work like collecting the rents (inspecting the proper-ty, contracting out any repairs, and renting out vacancies) you can further deduct this 'salary' from the income gener-ated from the property. One simple tip: open a separate bank account so you properly track all income and expens-es. Your accountant will love you for this by making their lives much easier. Save all receipts and track everything.

At the end of the four years, if you do not have another child attending university, you can sell it for a gain to pay off any student loans your child would have received, giving them an almost-free education! What you might want to do is put the house in the child's name to begin with so that when you do sell the home taxes will not have to be paid due to it being a principal residence (if your child is living there) and, because they will be a first-time homebuyer, you can get in with as little as 5% down.

Run an ad in the paper telling people how they can send their kids to school for free and just teach them to do what you did. Schedule an open house of the property and always schedule group showings as opposed to individual showings. This little act will create a sense of hype and urgency in people's minds and will allow you to get a maximum price for your home.

Rule #4
Leverage Time and Money

How to Keep the Dream from Dying

Today I will do what others won't so tomorrow I will accomplish what others cannot.
–Jerry Rice

కొ✑

Time Blocking

If I asked you who the most successful franchise is in the world today, you'd probably agree it would be McDonald's. Now, are they successful because of the food they make or the systems they follow? It's definitely not the food, as I know that if given a frozen pound of beef and a hot piece of Arizona asphalt, I could probably cook up a better burger than McDonald's! They are successful simply because of their turn-key systems that they have created over time.

To live your dream lifestyle and create your wealth deliberately is going to require that you have a daily systematic approach. Developing a routine will condition you to have the right actions that you can measure. The results will always be there so long as you have the activity. Many times people try to measure the results instead of the actions, which leaves them feeling frustrated and dream broke.

Blocking off time for work, family, fitness, community, personal, wealth and sleep will be the system you put in place so that you give yourself an opportunity to get done all that you need to do. Here's an example of mine. You'll notice that every morning I block time out for wealth. This is where I look at my bank and investment accounts, as well as yesterday's expenses. This keeps me in touch with money all the time. I know exactly where I stand at all times. I'll also use this time to see where my income is coming from and read up on the day's business news—just the highlights.

Another aspect to my time blocking is the way I follow-up with my e-mail and phone calls. I do it all as I head out of the office for the day. This allows me to create the space for my work to get done in the morning. Otherwise, I'd be responding all day and not getting any true work complete. Using this approach allows me to do what earns me money first and administration stuff second. My clients know this and respect it as it allows me to provide better service for them.

Give Yourself 15 Minutes

We are always rushed into and out of meetings. Do you ever get the feeling like you're not connected to people—just running around trying to get stuff done? Add 15 minutes to every meeting. If you are responsible for leading a team or serving clients, your meetings will become less frantic and you will learn so much more about who these people are in your life. In comparison, you'll show up as the person who is connected to them, wants to know who they are and has an interest in them. Ghandi said it best when he said, "Be the change." If you want your meetings to remain productive but want to feel more connected and less rushed, add 15 minutes and spend the time to learn more about these important people in your life or business. Use the time to enrich your life and add a sense of humanity to your day.

	Monday	Tuesday	Wednesday	Thursday	Friday	Saturday	Sunday
7	Wealth	Wealth	Wealth	Wealth	Wealth	Sleep	Sleep
8	Office	Office	Office	Office	Office	Sleep	Sleep
9	Office	Office	Office	Office	Office	Fitness	Life Plan
10	Office	Office	Office	Office	Office		Life Plan
11	Office	Office	Office	Office	Office		
12	Lunch	Lunch	Lunch	Lunch	Lunch	Lunch	Lunch
1	Office	Office	Office	Office	Office		
2	Office	Office	Office	Office	Office		
3	Dog	Fitness	Dog	Fitness	Dog		Fitness
4	Business Plan	Learn	Business Plan	Learn	Business Plan		
5	Home	Home	Home	Home	Home		
6	Dinner	Dinner	Dinner	Dinner	Dinner	Fun	Family
7	Connect				Personal	Fun	Family
8	Connect				Personal	Fun	Family
9	Personal	Personal	Personal	Personal	Personal	Fun	Personal
10	Journal	Journal	Journal	Journal	Journal	Fun	Journal
11	Sleep	Sleep	Sleep	Sleep	Sleep	Fun	Sleep

Stomping Out Multi-Tasking

You'll be amazed at how much you can get done when you focus on one thing at a time. By setting up the time block above, you deliberately create the space for everything to get done as it needs to get done throughout the course of the day. You will be less stressed, do better work which will improve your effectiveness. Imagine if a pitcher stood on the mound and replied to his SMS text, read his e-mail and was writing a report all the while he tried to deliver a fastball towards home plate! How is your work any different? To create true wealth requires discipline and in the zone-like focus.

Using Other People's Time, Money and Expertise

If you were to ask any millionaire if they used 100% of their own money to create the lifestyle they live, I'd guarantee each one of them would say 'no.' So many people try to do everything on their own that they end up nowhere closer to where they want to be.

This brings me to a great example that I can dig up from my days as a professional baseball umpire. It was my fourth professional plate job (calling balls and strikes) as a minor league umpire. We had just driven 275 miles from Medford, Oregon to Portland, Oregon and I was still excited, having been promoted from the Arizona League to the North West League just five days before. Medford was a small, dumpy little stadium, with uneven grass, and no formal locker room for the umpires. For the most part, we basically changed in the grounds-crew equipment shed...nice introduction to professional baseball. Portland was very different, a big stadium, excellent amenities and artificial turf. Even the crowds were bigger. This night we had over 20,000 people. Have you ever heard 20,000 people scream? Imagine if you were small enough and climbed your way into a cereal bowl and you had somebody scream into the bowl. That's what it's like being on the field; you can feel the pulse of the crowd in your chest, hair on end.

Late in the game, a ball was just hit over the outfield wall and into the seating and bounced back onto the field. An obvious home run to us so we ruled it as such. The Portland crowd wasn't too pleased thinking the ball had hit the wall; this brought out the Portland manager, Ron Guideon, onto the field to question what had just happened. After we managed to get Ron off the field, I remember seeing this one fan, all alone in the outfield seating, throwing a ball onto the field. Then, a moment later, another ball came onto the field from somewhere behind us and, before you knew it, baseballs were flying all over the place. In a heartbeat, 5,000 baseballs were now missiles and we were all running for cover—the players, and the umpires, everybody. As the plate umpire, I ran to the phone in the dugout to tell the PA guy to say something to stop the madness. I'd never seen anything like this.

It took 30 minutes to clean the field and calm the crowd to get the game back to normal. Turns out it was baseball give-away night. The first 5,000 fans were given a free baseball. Thank God this didn't happen the next night as it was free-miniature bat night. Out of common sense, the ball club gave them away after the game for fear of repeating the baseball incident.

What's amazing in all of this is how one person's actions can magnify an entire incident. To this day I still have the image of that one guy throwing that first baseball onto the field. The point of this whole story is that leveraging people, places and things allows you to get things done more quickly.

Other People's Time

If I could clone myself I would but, instead, I outsource and hire people to do the menial tasks in my life and in my business so I have more time to do the things I enjoy doing or that make me more money. I have a cleaning service to look after my condo, my car gets detailed while I work, my dog goes to dog day care three days a week and my groceries get delivered to my door. This frees up hours of valuable time for me and allows me to have a full weekend with family and friends and creates the space for productive creative work to get done Monday through Friday.

Other People's Money

Leveraged investing is a key principle in creating huge wealth, provided it's done conservatively. A great book to read is Talbot Steven's *Dispelling the Myths of Borrowing to Invest*. Whether it is a straight-up investment loan, a mortgage, using your home's equity to purchase a rental property, leveraging can collapse time frames for you. Imagine getting done in five years what you could achieve in 15. Always use a trusted advisor and understand that leveraging also magnifies your losses as much as it does your gains.

A solid financial advisor can create strategies where your tax deductions and refunds used in these concepts can be used to pay down the loan, making the idea even more attractive. You could even create the possibility of getting enough leveraged money invested for you today so that your retirement is completely looked after (providing good market returns). Imagine slam dunking your retirement in one-afternoon. This is what I've done and have done for many of my clients. By doing this we took care of one of the biggest concerns people have financially: will I have enough? By addressing this with leveraging, we can move onto the other elements of creating their dream lifestyle.

Lifestyle Strategy #7: Self-Directed Mortgage

Growing up in the real estate industry, I was exposed to buying and selling right from the get-go. My grandmother, Gerry Adair, was a long-standing top producer and broker/owner with RE/MAX and my mother ran the franchise, so I experienced the industry from many angles. From 1983 to 1989 we lived in seven houses.

Needless to say, I learned how to pack and move really well, too. Each new home was a brand new experience. We'd fix it up a bit and move on to the next one. If my parents had just a little more knowledge, they may have seen things differently. The last strategy I shared a way for you to create equity in your home. This chapter we're going to talk about taking that equity out of your home and diversifying it. This is not common logic, I know, but remember where common logic takes us—we don't want to end up in common logic land. Instead, we need to redefine what works and what doesn't work and this works. In Ric Edleman's book, *Ordinary People Extraordinary Wealth,* he says: "If you have a mortgage and you're dreaming of the day you're paying it off—you're doing something that financially successful people do not do!" Closer to home, Garth Turner says this in his book, *2015 After the Boom.* You should already be converting the equity in your home into liquid assets that will grow over the coming years."

If I gave you $250,000 today, would you go out and invest all of this money in one stock and hope that it grows and not tank? Not likely, yet everyday thousands of homeowners do this. They go to their lender, ask for $250,000 and plunk that money down on one investment which is not diversified at all. So they end up having a quarter of a million dollars sitting on one street, in one province, in one country. When you look at it from that perspective, how good of an idea is that? Any village idiot can figure that one out. That is why the last chapter is crucial for you to maximize your real estate because it is only when you have created equity in your home that your home has now become an investment. Before, it was just a leech on your financial growth.

There are several options that people can use to access the equity in their homes. The first one I will tell you not to use so we can get it out of the way. Despite the gracious media coverage it gets the reverse mortgage strategy is not your best bet. Reverse mortgages are often better for the lender than they are for the homeowner. The basics of a reverse mortgage are the lender will give you a lump sum (usually up to 40% of the value of your home) and charge you interest on it and much higher than conventional mortgage rates I might add. Usually your home has to be paid off but that is not the case for all reverse mortgages. There are no payment requirements but the problem lies within the compounding interest as it will erode your leftover equity as the principal does not decrease but rather it increases over time. There are also age restrictions as the reverse mortgage is meant for seniors. A secured line of credit is a much better route to go, ignore the hype.

If you've been in the housing market for a while now, you have probably experienced some nice growth. Homes all across Canada have increased in value as that means more homeowners are sitting on equity that is not diversified and not working for them. I want you to think of your equity as a bar of gold underneath the floor boards collecting dust. Meanwhile, your home is still quietly appreciating in value. Until you unlock the equity it's just sitting there dormant, sleeping and hoping to be woken up sometime soon. Once you wake it up and put it to work in either more real estate or other investments, it doesn't appreciate, how can it, as it has not been put to work? The beautiful thing is once you get the equity out working for you, you now have two investments rather than one.

If your home is paid for how, would feel to really be able to live the dream life? I see this lot in Vancouver; couples living in Kitsilano where they bought their home for $30,000 back in the 1960's and now the house is worth over one million dollars. Money just sitting there is doing nothing. If this is you, you should borrow against it and use those monies to create an income for yourself. The interest on the new line of credit will be tax deductible and you could literally be travelling the world every year!

Average Property Values

City	1997	2010
Vancouver	$285,000	$638,000
Calgary	$141,000	$382,000
Saskatoon	$96,766	$142,741
Regina	$82,000	$214,000
Toronto	$208,000	$409,000
Ottawa	$141,000	$324,000
Halifax	$107,000	$242,000
St. John's	$87,000	$164,000

Source: Canadian Real Estate Association

There are a few things you can do with equity in your home. The first strategy that I will show you is using a secured line of credit to replace your existing mortgage. The second and third strategy we will look at other real estate investments.

When you refinance your present mortgage with a new secured line of credit (Home Equity Line of Credit or HELOC), you are only required to pay back the interest each month. By doing this you become in control and not the lender. In a traditional mortgage, you make two payments. They come out on the same day as one payment but essentially it's two. One is for the interest and the other is for the principal; they are blended so you don't know the difference. Under HELOC, you separate the interest payment from the principal payment...the lender won't even ask you for the principal payment. Instead of giving them your principal payment each month, you are going to pay it to yourself in a quality investment—we'll discuss that in a minute—over the same duration as your mortgage. So, your cash flow does not change, just who is getting the money and where the money ends up changes. Of course, with this strategy if you are paying yourself the principal payment, your principal balance is not going to go down. I repeat not going to go down, this is a good thing because you will be able to be better by being in control of this yourself. Remember what Ric Edelman said, "The wealthy don't pay down their mortgages...so we're just going to copy the wealth in this instance."

Now, depending on how much equity you've created, there will be a chunk of money that you can still access because you can go as high as 75% of the appraised value of your home. So, if you had a $200,000 home, you could obtain a HELOC agreement for $150,000. Let's say you owed $100,000, you would then have $50,000 still to access from the line of credit. This $50,000 is the equity portion that you will invest; again, I'll touch on 'in what' in a minute. The moment we draw this $50,000 from the line of credit, we will have to pay interest on it. Assuming a prime lending rate of 5%, you would owe $208 each month in interest which is tax deductible. When we borrow money to invest in income-generating property, we can deduct the interest cost associated with that investment loan. Now, there are two ways to pay this interest charge each month. The first way is out of your pocket...keep in mind we lowered your monthly payment on the mortgage side because you are now only paying the interest each month and not the principal. Another way to pay this is to have the investment pay for this each month. That's right; you can literally borrow money and not have it cost you a cent of your own cash. By setting up a systematic withdrawal plan or SWP each month, you can have the investment withdraw $208 and deposit it into your chequing account each month to cover this interest cost.

Once it's set up, everything runs automatically, just like it did when you had your mortgage. The same cash flow each month is just restructured, more like a monthly investment as opposed to a monthly bill, putting you in control of your wealth and your future. There is a better strategy to maximize your real estate than the HELOC strategy. If you wanted to run a more conservative approach to this because you would not be able to sleep at night knowing that you're not paying down the principal each month, then continue to pay it down but still get your equity out using the same HELOC strategy so you can maximize the equity you've created.

Always get a secured line of credit that is at or below prime and non-callable. You want a non-callable line of credit that has no annual reviews. For easy accounting, I would also have the lender split up the line of credit so that you can have one for the debt side and one for the equity side; your accountant will love you for this. Every few years, you can always renegotiate your line of credit as property values increase to access more equity and continue to increase your portfolio.

There are some downsides to this strategy. The first one is interest rates. If interest rates rise, well, so do our payments and also our tax deduction on the investment side of the strategy. If you ever get nervous, you can always flip it over to a conventional loan and know that your rates are locked in. Doing this though, you will have to pay back the principal payments each month. Also remember this, if prime is at 5% and you're in a 50% tax bracket, your true interest cost is only 2.5%—I call this crazy money. The other risk is the investment risk. If the investment doesn't outperform the cost of borrowing, we're hooped to put it mildly. Don't fret, this is a long-term strategy and there are many great managed portfolio products out there that have rebalancing to make sure that your investment tool is tuned up every month to win the race. If you're leery about mutual funds, consider segregated funds. They have to guarantee your principal at a minimum of 75%; most have an option for 100% over a ten-year period. Segregated funds also allow you to reset your guarantees, so if your portfolio grew from $50,000 to $65,000 in three years, you can 'reset' the

$65,000 over another ten years. This is a great way to ladder and secure your growth. There are also some great estate strategies with segregated funds because you need to name a beneficiary; this way they can by-pass probate fees. Some great segregated fund portfolios can be found through your trusted advisor.

The other investment you can utilize is real estate. Instead of investing in financial assets, you could invest in real assets like a rental condo or investment property or land banking, which is becoming more accessible and mainstream. You won't be as diversified but you could duplicate what you did on your principal residence and create another tool to generate more income for you now and down the road. Imagine living in a paid-off home and having another property giving you $1,500 a month income… plus any interest costs and expenses you can use to lower your taxable income.

Other People's Expertise

There are many experts out there who have the answers and resources I need that I can get access quickly, where, if on my own, could take hours of time and possibly months or years to learn. I always use a mortgage broker and not a lender at a bank; they can get me the best and have more room to be creative and negotiate on my behalf. A lender at a bank has one option and is paid a salary—one that might not motivate them to get the deal done.

If I were not an independent financial advisor not working at a bank-owned or insurance company-owned financial firm, I'd be sure to align myself with one. The reason is that they can represent the entire industry, as opposed to one company and their bag of products. I would receive unbiased advice, not tied to company sales campaigns or incentives and know I have the best of the best in my portfolio. Who manages your money and your financial plan? Here are some key questions to consider:

1. Does your financial advisor sell only proprietary products from their parent firm? If yes, they don't represent your best interest nor can they find you the best products.

2. Aside from your financial advisor offering you mutual funds, do they have the capacity and licensing to offer you segregated funds, Exchange Traded Funds (ETFs), stocks and bonds? If not, how do you know you have the best and most suitable investments in your portfolio?

3. Can your advisor offer you fee-only service? If no, then consider the "advice" you are getting. Remember, the "advice" you're getting will only go as far as the products your advisor can sell you!

Other experts are travel agents, lawyers, telemarketers, general insurance brokers, and personal coaches.

Other People's Expertise—The Seven Things My Grandfather Taught Me about Being Wealthy

Bill Kurtz wasn't my blood grandfather. He was my grandmother's second husband. I called him Bill and he certainly was all that a grandfather was supposed to be, a buddy, a mentor, a true hero for me. The guy didn't have it easy. He came from a broken home and wasn't the healthiest lad during the depression. He tried to join the Canadian Armed Forces only because he was hungry; there wasn't much work and he loved to eat. He wasn't accepted so he turned to the logging industry in BC and worked in camps and learned as he went. He told me of a time when he set foot in a camp and the foreman asked him if he knew how to work a cat. He said 'of course' and, in a few seconds, figured it out—he needed that pay cheque to fill his tummy. Anyhow, the guy had a grand sense of character and really epitomizes much of this book. I used to look after his yard and he'd share these stories with me and, always, lessons of money. Here are some that I can recollect:

1. Treat Yourself Like a Portfolio
Investment portfolios follow a set diversified mix are reviewed often and get rebalanced when things are not in alignment. The same methodology can be used in your life. Whether it is your health, your work, business or hobbies. Keep yourself and them in check and don't let anything run away from you. By keeping your life fine-tuned, the harmony your life creates will always be a song that attracts birds instead of keeping them afar.

2. Tuck Away Spare Change

We all love surprises and creating something from nothing is a great surprise. Loose change is always floating around, harness those coins and put them to work in abundance by saving them for something special every year.

3. Reflect on Your Goals and Vision

It doesn't matter your religion or faith. What does matter is you take the time to visualize your path, acknowledge your maker and don't let life get so busy you lose your compass in all of the shuffle.

4. Keep Work Work

Mixing your personal and professional lives means you're never really present in either. Being present is where you allow yourself to create in the moment, keep the files at the office and don't get too relaxed around the water cooler.

5. Seek Independence From Money

A job gives you security in a pay cheque every two weeks but has you shackled to someone else's dream. See ways to create passive income so your dreams can breathe, your time becomes your own and you live for you.

6. Set Your Financial Standards

Earning more money is often spent the same day it's earned if you haven't set financial standards for yourself. True wealth can be created with greater ease if you exercise a sense of frugality and patience.

7. Break Your Business Down

Knowing your numbers is the greatest indicator that you are on the court as a captain and not in the stands as a raving fan. Don't be a raving fan of your business, know the numbers and work them as you need to in order to deliberately create the success your business needs so your life can live the life you most desperately want it to live.

The real point to sharing my lessons from Bill is that you never know where life's lessons will come from or who will be the teacher. In either case I was ready and they both showed up because I allowed them to. I cast no judgement with them, placed no expectations, and just created them both in the moment which allowed them to show up in my life fully self-expressed. When you create the space of allowing others to be fully self-expressed in your presence, divine things happen there on the spot in that moment of creation. The act of allowing is selfless; by putting this act into effect, you earn the right to be selfish.

Exercise: Take a friend for coffee and cast aside any previous judgements or limitations you ever placed on them as a friend. View them as whole, complete and perfect. See how the conversation goes. To take it a step further, when you sit down, tell them that you've cast all this aside and then really see where this truly authentic conversation goes.

Leverage Your Time—Do Just Two More

In 2007, I took this on for myself in the gym: 'just two more' and earned the physique I was aiming for. That spilled over into other areas of my life as well. On the phone calling prospects, following up with existing clients, studying for industry-related exams, playing with the dog, whatever it was, I committed to doing just two more. It didn't matter what it was but I increased my productivity in all areas of my life by 20% without spending any more additional time really as I was already in motion. I was already on the phone, on the treadmill, throwing sticks, reading the book.

Yet, if I took on the challenge of increasing the productivity in my life by 20% I'd have failed. Unreachable, too much time, too stressed...excuses would have prevailed. Instead, it's easier to keep in motion what already is in motion, so do just two more and you'll be amazed at your results and how your life can change. If all you took away from this book was 'just two more' then you'll have received your money's worth. Please share this book or this principle with two more people at work—thanks!

Becoming Financially Independent

My final season in professional baseball had been a long season for both my umpire partner Steve Corvi and me. On the field life was pretty solid. We worked extremely well together, earned the respect of most managers and had fun at the same time. Off the field well, that tended to be a bit of a struggle. The league president, Joe Gagliardi, had the reputation of not going to bat for his umpires and essentially just not caring. Steve's mom was going through some treatment for breast cancer back in New York so he needed to go home and be with her. Looking at our schedule, we were to be working two series in Rancho Cugomongo, with a day off in between the two series. Rancho is right near the Ontario airport so it made it real easy for Steve to get back and for me to get him to and from the airport. So, looking at our schedule, he asked for seven days off, as on the fifth day, we had a regularly scheduled off day. Most prudent people understanding the situation would have said take as much time as you need. Instead, Gagliardi insisted Steve be back on the day before our day off. Gagliardi's decision was based totally on his control of our world, knowing if we went to our supervisors, they could not really give a damn about us. Minor league umpires for the most part, fend for themselves. So, instead of getting an extra day and half with his mom, Steve was forced to fly back and spend the off day in the smog-filled city of Rancho Cugomongo. That was life in the California League and not even the half of it.

Our season was ending in a small town outside Temecula, California called Lake Ellsinore. This little Mayberry-like town of Lake Ellsinore is nestled in behind the mountains just north of San Diego. On a lake, this place had an ambience all of its own. What was once the crystal-meth corridor of California is now a baseball proud town of a few thousand people. Had it not been for the crack-house conditions we stayed in Lake Elsinor, it would have easily been the best city in the Cal league. The stadium was brand new and absolutely beautiful—owned by Mandalay Entertainment; it had big-league locker rooms and all the amenities.

You'd think that with all this money and nearby hotels, the club would show some respect to its umpires and opposing teams.

The Lake Elsinore Hotel and Casino was hell above ground and open to the public. Driving up, you see an old motor lodge looking over the lake. And you knew that in its day, it was the best place in town. We had been here four times before this stay so we knew what we were in for.

Previous crews had found blood on the sheets, drug paraphernalia, and even a snake! Nothing was a surprise. The phones didn't work and sometimes the doors didn't either. Had it not been for a full bottle of Febreze being sprayed on the carpet, curtains, lampshades, and beds, one could easily vomit from the nicotine-drenched fabrics covering the room. The bedspreads always came off to be used as an area rug so as to keep as much distance from you and the carpet. The towels—we always took towels from the stadium—and tried to shower as much as possible either at the stadium or at the gym in town. This place was not sanitary in the least. At one point we almost slept in our truck for fear of catching something from these rooms.

Occasionally, we'd end up in the hotel lobby bar before crashing out for the night. But even that was an experience. We called it the 'Star Wars bar.' Inside the hotel was a small 12 x 15 foot-lounge filled with smoke and the original bartender, Smitty who, as always, was fully loaded by the time we got there. The whole room couldn't fit more than 20 people at a time, had a low ceiling, red leather booths, and even red lighting. Had it not been for the mirrors on the walls, you probably would have been claustrophobic. The music was supplied through an old jukebox with a broken speaker and, when that went down, Smitty always had the 8-track under the counter ready to go in case of emergencies. Remember this is in 1999. You never knew who was going to be there as the casino was right next door; there was always a character or two who was in between losing hands or needing to flood their brain with more whisky to sustain their evening.

For this final series my brother had decided to come down to see me on the road and drive me back home after this series. After the final game myself, my brother and Steve went back to the Star Wars bar to down a few beers and talk about the season and to contemplate if we were both going to come back to baseball or not. Getting bored with this literal hole-in-the-wall bar, we decided to get out of there and go to another bar call the 'Out Back Bar.' We had neglected to go there all season and thought with my brother in town we had best check it out to change things a bit. Within walking distance, we marched over to this place that was tucked in behind some trees. Outside a few Harleys rested and music was pumping out the door. Next to the door stood a mammoth of a man who was obviously the bouncer and gatekeeper. Once we made it in, we quickly realized that we were the only three guys wearing khakis in this whole place, so we rushed to the bar and bought some beer, which was the coldest beer I have ever had in my life.

The bar was a room of an old house and 'sketchy' doesn't begin to describe this place. The lights were really dim and a pool table took up most of the room. The room was so tight for space that all of the pool cues had been sawed down so that guys could make their shot without putting a hole in the wall. It was definitely a biker bar and to see bikers playing pool with short sticks was something to see. Biting my lip I said nothing and took in this place. My eyes finally made their way to a dark corner where I could see a female dancing, attempting to provide some level of low-grade amateur entertainment. We were eventually able to bring ourselves fully inside the bar, but had to position ourselves closer to this dingy corner. While our eyes adjusted to the light, we noticed that this lady had to have been in her late 50's. She was dancing on a crate with a two-by-four as the pole! Seriously! She was very weathered, had long, streaky, blonde-grey hair and a lengthy C-section scar. Her eyes were rolling around in her head like a set of marbles. Seeing this, I knew we had to down our beer and go, and we did. Walking away confused and bewildered not sure what we had just seen; we all knew this would create for a great epic story for years to come. It was called the 'Out Back Bar,' because the bathrooms, which were outhouses, were literally out back!

My night was over and so was the 1999 season. On the ride home with my brother the next day, I decided that my career as a professional umpire too was going to be over. We all have moments in our lives where we reach a place and wonder where the heck am I? How in the world did I end up here? Is this for real? Is it worth being treated like this? Will it get any better?

When it comes to people's finances, I see this every day. People plot along with no plan, thinking everything will be all right and then life smacks them in the face and they're left standing holding the pieces of a broken puzzle. Or, worse yet, they just hope things will improve maybe some-day. Someday isn't coming folks.

Imagine retiring today with no plan and no financial knowl-edge. How many days would you last? People take this life event for granted. We tend to put more effort into plan-ning a family vacation than to plan our financial future and it's because most people don't know what to do, where to start, what questions to ask and who to seek counsel with.

Without the right plan, you will spend your retirement years in a land of paradox and uncertainty, much like my time spent in Lake Ellsinore and the characters that made up the story. You'll feel like your world is spiralling down-ward and you have no control on how fast you're falling. The difference to Lake Ellsinore is that I wasn't in control of being assigned there but I was in control of how I adapted, and adjusted my environment so that I could feel more comfortable. For you, your retirement years are no differ-ent. You will end up in a scary place if you do not create, implement and monitor your financial and life plan and take action today.

Roughly, 71% of people who retire at the age of 65, will retire financially challenged earning less than $50K a year. The reason is simply not enough retirement savings. Many will be dependent, relying on those Social Security or CPP/OAS payments from the government, while others may find themselves taking on unwanted part-time or, even worse, full-time work to increase their cash flow. With the proper planning and consistency in savings, this can all be avoided. The key is having a plan, working that plan and then reviewing it often with financial professionals. It's great to have a dream lifestyle plan and a call to action to achieve those dreams but, at the same time, becoming financially unrepentant needs to be on the list. You need to be rich or you will have to continue to work and be capped by your income, I don't want that for you. This life is too short to be spending it working for money. You'll see being financially independent by age 45 is on the top of my list.

Here are some things you can do to figure out how much money you'll need to become financially secure:

a) Decide on a realistic age you will stop needing to be dependent on working.

b) Figure out in today's dollars what your retirement lifestyle would require. The easiest way to do this is to look at it from a monthly perspective and multiply that number by 12. Now remember much of your debts will no longer be around. We also have a free download on-line to help you determine your future dream lifestyle expenses.

c) Next, go use my Deliberate Wealth Calculator on-line to get your financial independence number. **www.deliberatewealth.com**

Your FIN# is a snapshot of your current financial picture. Obviously, if your income increases or decreases, your FIN# will change just as well. I often recommend to my clients they assume that they are retired today. We write out a list of all that they'd like to do and associate a dollar amount for that experience. For instance, if they want to golf twice a week, join a gym, or travel three times a year, we figure out roughly what that's going to cost in today's dollars, factor in some living expenses, emergency funds and create an annual retirement income that way, instead of using what they are presently earning. Either way, you will have the framework to begin savings toward your goal and so you can experience a full life after working.

≈∼≈

Rule #5
Make Sure Others Get It and Have Fun Along The Way

Enrolling Others and Helping Friends

You will get all you want in life if you help enough other people get what they want.—Zig Ziglar

෬ ෪

Life is not a journey to the grave with intentions of arriving safely in a pretty well-preserved body, but rather to skid in broadside, thoroughly used-up, totally worn out and loudly proclaiming…"WOW! What a ride!"

You never really arrive anywhere unless you share the journey with someone else. The concept of paying it forward enriches your life and the lives around you. If we all practised a random act of kindness each day and propelled that from one person to another, the world would be a much different place.

There are many ways in which you can share yourself, your knowledge and your experiences. I'd like to first request that you share this book with those whom you respect and admire and let it be known with them what you are up to in your life. Junior Achievement is a wonderful organization where successful people donate their time in teaching the youth in our communities about business, life, the arts, to help them gain new perspectives and insights from those who have done it already. Chances are your church or community groups would be open to having you work with them in sharing yourself and what you are good at.

Purposefully, I am selfish when it comes to my spending time with people. I need to have positive successful people around me always. It doesn't matter if it's personally or professionally I choose to ignite the fire within those around me and spend my time with those who can ignite mine. The difference of where I am today and where I was five years ago comes down to two things. The books I've read and the people I've included in my circle. I've taken on the belief that the right people always come into my life at the right time. Since allowing this declaration to manifest, I have been blessed to have experienced both the student and the teacher with many dynamic, charismatic people from all over the globe making my life truly fantabulous!

Having Fun

Purpose and laughter are the twins that must not separate.
Each is empty without the other.
—Robert K. Greenleaf

Louis Carragio, a successful personal trainer from New York reminded me that fun can be the centre of all things and when you place fun as intent, an exciting shift in one's life will take place. When he first shared this with me he reminded me of my fourth-grade teacher telling my mom that she had the oldest fourth-grader in the class, meaning I was an old soul. Even to this day, I can get caught up in the 'seriousness' conundrum of life and business as good as the next guy. Louis asked me one question:**"If you made it a point to have a fun/work environment, how would that affect your firm, your clients and your life outside of work?"** Immediately avalanches of possibilities were being invented for me on the spot. In sharing yourself and enrolling others, fun can be the underpinning of it all. After all, if life and work is not fun, what else is there? This was a pleasant reminder that life is meant to be fun, it's a game and games are played to put a smile in our lives so add it to your day and to the day of those around you.

Exercise: Identify three things you can add to your week to make it more fun. Look at areas in your life that seem to be a struggle, wear you down or burden your day. Couple this with the paradigm shift converter from the first chapter and experience the source of fun.

૭ન્ઐ

The Realities of a Dream

It's never too late to be what you might have been.
—George Eliot

ॐॐ

The irony in all of this pursuit is that there is nowhere to go but where you are right now. The difference between today and tomorrow since your buying and following this book is the way you will now experience the journey or the process of 'getting there.' How will you know you've arrived? Is it the money in your account, the toys you have, the trips you've taken, or the more authentic relationships you'll create? Those will all show up as evidence of your having received. Received, that to deliberately create your dream lifestyle takes authenticity of a new kind. From your relationship with yourself, others and how you react to emotions and upsets along the way is all a game, now you know the rules and a have a few strategies to help you deliberately create the wealth and lifestyle of which you dream.

Enthusiastically,
Tyler Hoffman

ॐॐ